Title: You Can't Ride the Subway In Your Pajamas!
Published by Chanticlare Press, NYC.

Summary: A story about Sammy, who loves trains,
delaying bedtime and imagining all the NYC subway
adventures he could go on instead of going to sleep.

By Brad Spiegel
Illustrations & Artwork by Giovanni Mattucci & Aliza Lewis.

First published in 2017.
Copyright ©2017. All Rights Reserved.
ISBN 978-0-578-18874-4
Printed in South Korea.

You Can't Ride The Subway In Your Pajamas!

For my wife Jessica, my daughter Sloane and my son Sammy,
who loves to ride the New York City subway.

"Sammy, it's pajama time!"

Sammy loves trains. He knows all of the subway lines that make up the New York City Transit System.

He loves learning about the different stops each train makes and pointing out all the subway stations nearby.

"Union Square has the
N, Q, R *and* the 4, 5, 6!

The L train goes across
14th Street to Brooklyn!"

Sammy is so proud that he
knows where each train goes.

He loves riding in the first car
and looking at the tunnel ahead so
he can pretend he is driving the train.

He loves pretending to be
the train conductor and saying,

"Stand clear of the
closing doors, please!"

But one thing Sammy *does not like* is BEDTIME.
He would do ANYTHING to delay bedtime.

Each night, as he puts on his pajamas,
Sammy asks if he can take a quick subway
ride just to delay going to sleep!

"Mommy, can we take the
6 train to Grand Central Station?

I love to see all the people
rushing to the big
Metro-North trains!"

"Oh Sammy,"said his mommy,

"I'd love to take you on the
6 train, but you can't ride
the subway in your pajamas!"

Just as Sammy was about to hop into his bed, he ran to his mommy and asked,

"Mommy, can we take the 2 train to The Bronx Zoo to see the animals?"

"Sammy, you can't ride the subway in your pajamas!"

This made Sammy giggle.

5 AV Subway Station

N R W

"Mommy, can we take
the R train to Central Park?

We can watch the little
sailboats and have a picnic!"

"Or can we take the C train to
The Museum of Natural History?
I love learning about the dinosaurs.
ROAR!"

"Sammy, I'd love to take you
to Central Park and The Museum
of Natural History, but you can't
ride the subway in your pajamas!"

Sammy then quietly
approached his daddy.

"Daddy, can we take the N train
to Brooklyn to The Transit Museum?

I love looking out the window
and seeing The Brooklyn Bridge!"

"Or can we take a ride on the 7 train
to Citi Field to see the Mets play?"

"Sammy, I'd love to take you to
The Transit Museum and to Citi Field,
but you can't ride the subway
in your pajamas.

Plus, the Mets aren't playing
a night game tonight."

With a big smile, Sammy then took his mommy and daddy by the hand.

"Mommy, Daddy, can we go on the Q train to Coney Island to ride The Cyclone?"

His parents smiled and said,

"Sammy, you know you can't ride the subway in your pajamas!"

Now, Sammy could not stop giggling.

Then Sammy's daddy picked him up
in his arms and said,

"OK, Mister, it is time for bed and if
you close your eyes and go to sleep,
then tomorrow we can ride any train
you want...just not in your pajamas!"

They all laughed together as Sammy closed his eyes and went to sleep dreaming of all the fun they would have tomorrow.

GOOD
NIGHT